For Parker and Karen

This hardback edition published in 2020. First published in 2015 by Flying Eye Books,
an imprint of Nobrow Ltd. 27 Westgate Street, London E8 3RL.

Text and Illustrations © Keith Negley 2015.
Keith Negley has asserted his right under the Copyright, Designs and Patents Act,
1988, to be identified as the Author and Illustrator of this Work.

7 9 10 8

Published in the US by Nobrow (US) Inc.
Printed in Poland on FSC® certified paper.

ISBN: 978-1-909263-66-6
www.flyingeyebooks.com

Keith Negley

TOUGH GUYS

(Have Feelings Too)

Flying Eye Books

London | Los Angeles

It's not always easy being
a tough guy...

You might not think it, but tough guys have feelings too.

Even when they're with their best friends,

or when they're on top of the world,

not everything works out.

This can be very frustrating.

No matter how strong,

or fast,

or brave they are.

Everyone has feelings,

well... most of us anyway!

And it's ok to show them...

...just like these tough guys,
who love each other very much.